Title Withdrawn

# I Know a Shy Fellow Who Swallowed a Cello

by **Barbara S. Garriel**

**Illustrated by**
**John O'Brien**

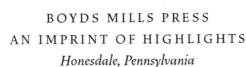

BOYDS MILLS PRESS
AN IMPRINT OF HIGHLIGHTS
*Honesdale, Pennsylvania*

For my mom, Helen F. Schmitz, thank you for those first piano lessons.
For my husband, Freddie
In memory of Eunice Johnson and Margaret McGlinn, my piano teachers
—*BSG*

For my favorite piano player, Tess
—*JO'B*

Publisher Cataloging-in-Publication Data (U.S.)

Garriel, Barbara.
  I know a shy fellow who swallowed a cello / by Barbara Garriel ;
illustrated by John O'Brien. —1st ed.
[32] p. : col. ill. ; cm.
Summary: An adaptation of the folk rhyme "There was an old woman who
swallowed a fly," featuring musical instruments.
ISBN: 978-1-59078-043-5 (hc)
ISBN: 978-1-59078-946-9 (pb)
1. Violoncello — Fiction. 2. Humorous stories. 3. Stories in rhyme.
I. O'Brien, John, 1953– ill. II. Title.
  [E] 21  PZ8.3.G377Ik 2004
2003108160

Text copyright © 2004 by Barbara S. Garriel
Illustrations copyright © 2004 by John O'Brien
All rights reserved.
For information about permission to reproduce
selections from this book, please contact
permissions@highlights.com.

Boyds Mills Press, Inc.
An Imprint of Highlights
815 Church Street
Honesdale, Pennsylvania 18431
Printed in China

First edition
The text of this book is set in 17-point Celeste Antiqua.

10 9 8 7 6 5 4

I KNOW A SHY FELLOW . . .

. . .WHO SWALLOWED A CELLO.

I don't know why he swallowed a cello.
Perhaps he'll bellow.

I know a shy fellow who swallowed a harp.
Not so sharp, to swallow a harp.
He swallowed the harp to jam with the cello.
I don't know why he swallowed the cello.
Perhaps he'll bellow.

I know a shy fellow who swallowed a sax.
Hard to relax, when you swallow a sax.
He swallowed the sax to jam with the harp.

He swallowed the harp to jam with the cello.
I don't know why he swallowed the cello.
Perhaps he'll bellow.

I know a shy fellow who swallowed a fiddle.

No time to twiddle, when you swallow a fiddle.

He swallowed the fiddle to jam with the sax.

He swallowed the sax to jam with the harp.

He swallowed the harp to jam with the cello.

I don't know why he swallowed the cello.

Perhaps he'll bellow.

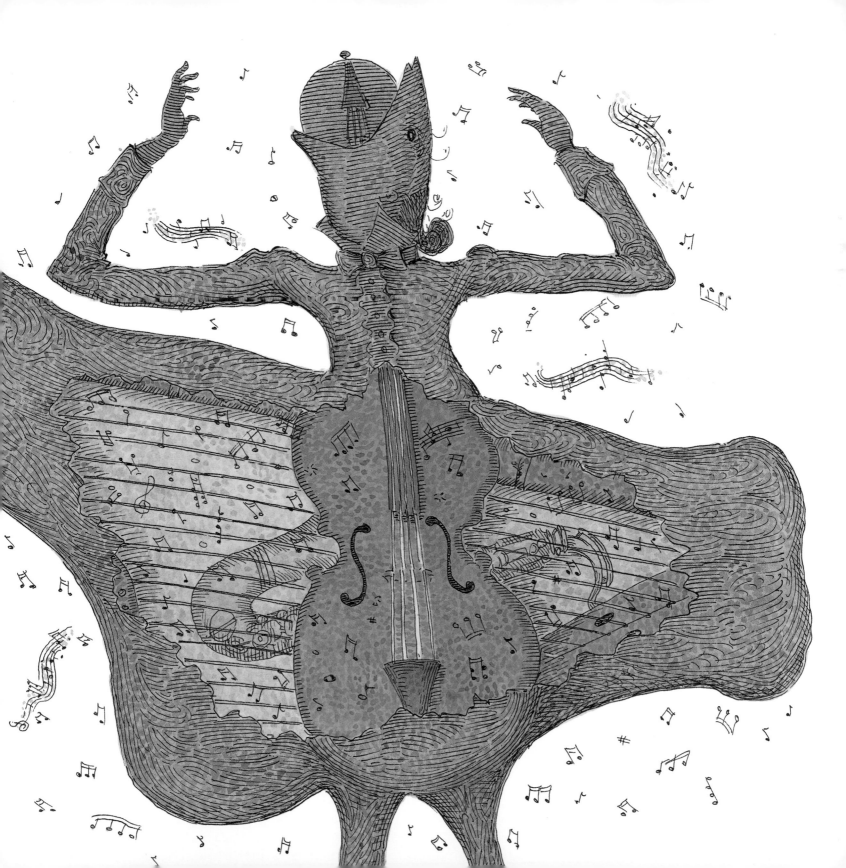

I know a shy fellow who swallowed a cymbal.

Not so nimble, to swallow a cymbal.

He swallowed the cymbal to jam with the fiddle.

He swallowed the fiddle to jam with the sax.

He swallowed the sax to jam with the harp.

He swallowed the harp to jam with the cello.

I don't know why he swallowed the cello.

Perhaps he'll bellow.

I know a shy fellow who swallowed a flute.

That was a hoot, to swallow a flute.

He swallowed the flute to jam with the cymbal.

He swallowed the cymbal to jam with the fiddle.

He swallowed the fiddle to jam with the sax.
He swallowed the sax to jam with the harp.
He swallowed the harp to jam with the cello.
I don't know why he swallowed the cello.
Perhaps he'll bellow.

I know a shy fellow who swallowed a kazoo.

Strange thing to do, swallow a kazoo.

He swallowed the kazoo to jam with the flute.

He swallowed the flute to jam with the cymbal.

He swallowed the cymbal to jam with the fiddle.

He swallowed the fiddle to jam with the sax.
He swallowed the sax to jam with the harp.
He swallowed the harp to jam with the cello.
I don't know why he swallowed the cello.
Perhaps he'll bellow.

I know a shy fellow who swallowed a bell.
The teeniest, tiniest, petite cascabel.

WELL . . .

His belly it wiggled, his belly did shake.
It rumbled and tumbled, it quivered and quaked.

It rocked and it rolled, it swivelled and swelled.
And all on account of that wee little bell.

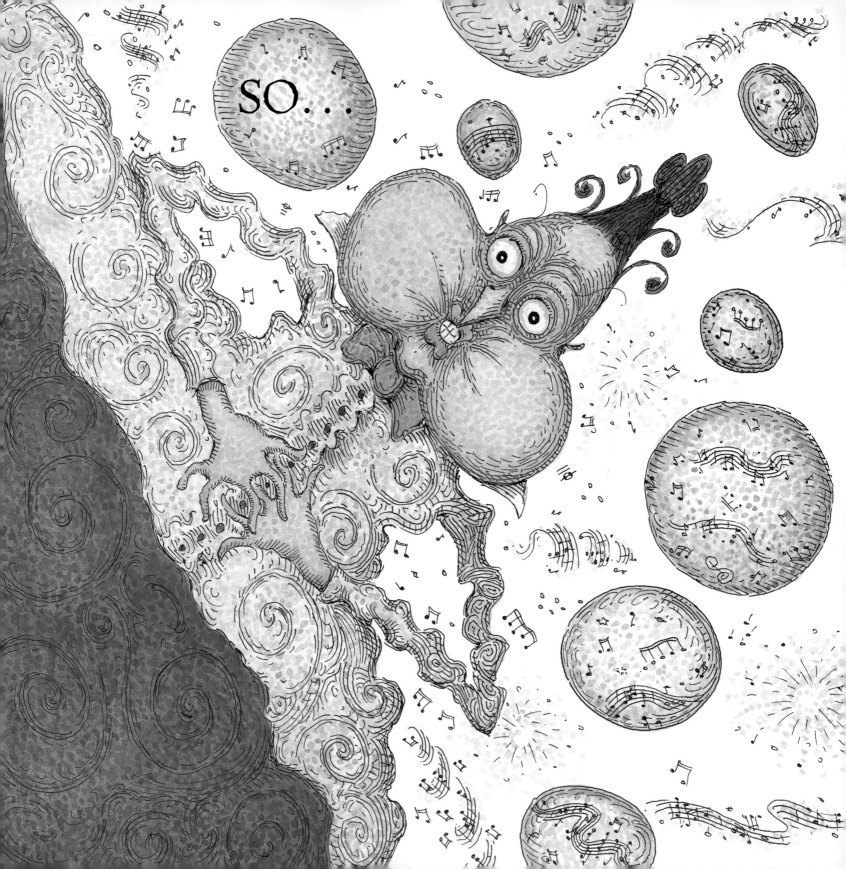

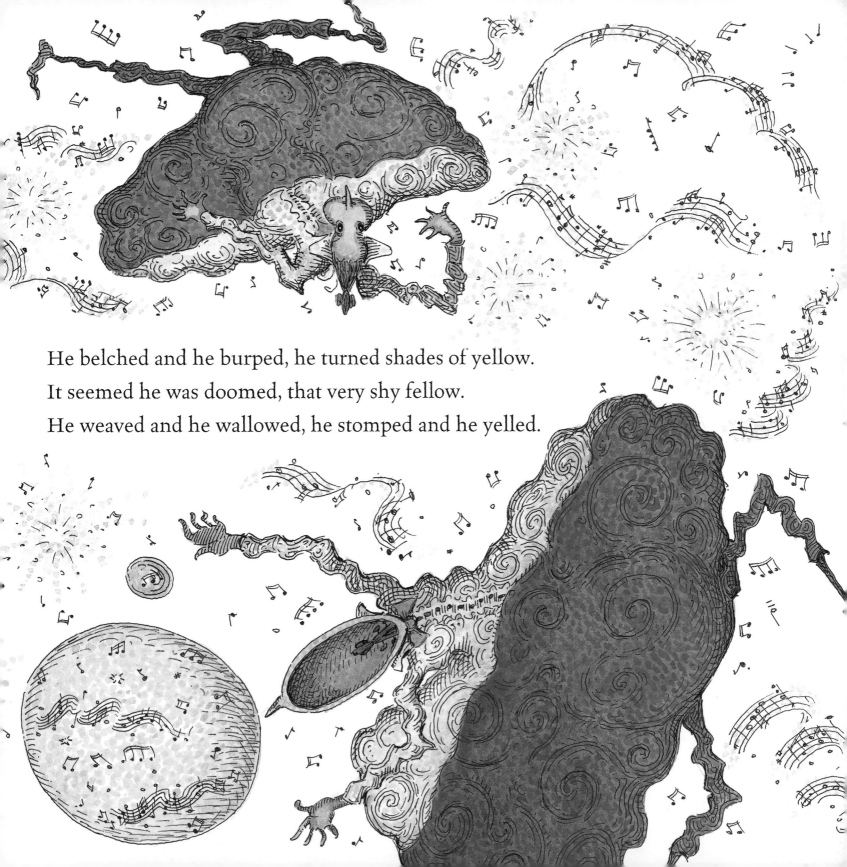

He belched and he burped, he turned shades of yellow.
It seemed he was doomed, that very shy fellow.
He weaved and he wallowed, he stomped and he yelled.

AND THE NEXT THING HE KNEW,
OUT JINGLED THE BELL.

THEN . . .

Out buzzed the kazoo,
out tooted the flute,

out crashed the cymbal.
That noisy galoot!

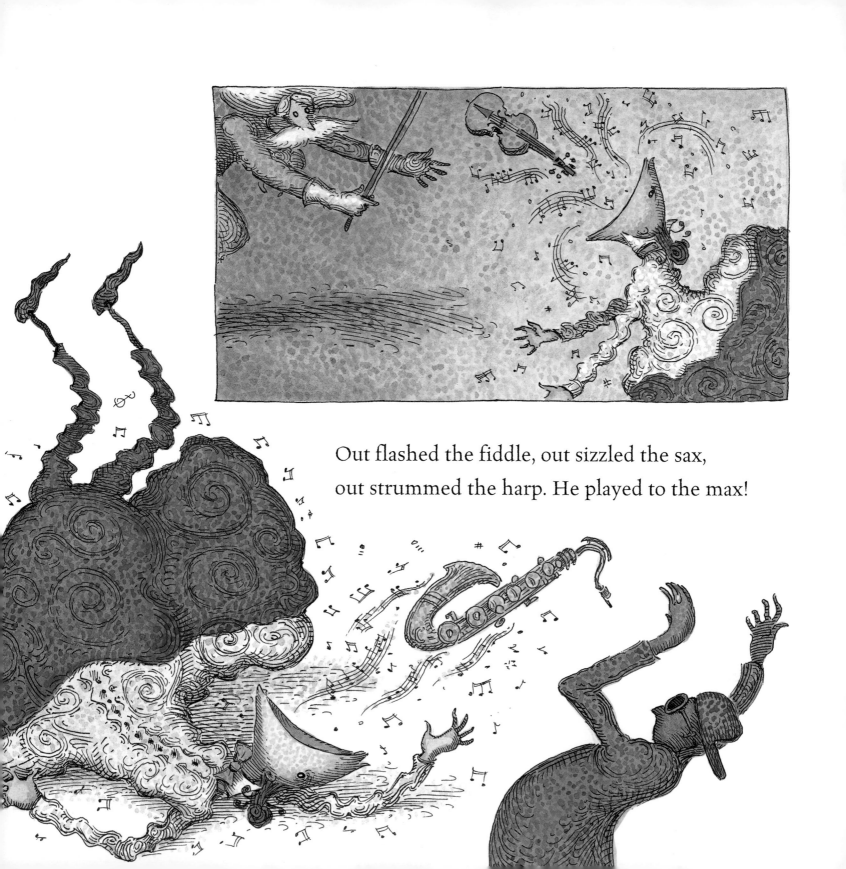

Out flashed the fiddle, out sizzled the sax,
out strummed the harp. He played to the max!

Well, he bellowed, that fellow,
that fellow did bellow . . .

. . . and last but not least,
out cha-chaed the cello!